BOBBIE'S GIRL

BOBBIE'S GIRL

BETTY STRACHAN

Order this book online at www.trafford.com
or email orders@trafford.com

Most Trafford titles are also available at major online book retailers.

FIRST EDITION

Printed in the United States of America.

ISBN: 978-1-4669-3845-8 (sc)
ISBN: 978-1-4669-3844-1 (e)

Trafford rev. 07/28/2012

 www.trafford.com

North America & international
toll-free: 1 888 232 4444 (USA & Canada)
phone: 250 383 6864 ✦ fax: 812 355 4082

CONTENTS

ACKNOWLEDGEMENT

I want to express my sincere thanks to my mother who encouraged me to write poems and stories when I was eight years old and show gratitude to Mrs. Caroline Johnson my directing teacher at Charles Drew Elementary for writing and producing plays for the students there. She motivated me to write and produce my first play titled "Over the Rainbow" at Auburndale Elem., Miami, Florida. Fond appreciation is extended to Principal Roger Shatanof for giving me the opportunity to write and produce this play at Auburndale, and a touch of gratefulness to all of them.

DEDICATION

To people who have been abused by others they trusted and loved.

This book is dedicated to my husband Eddie and sister Ruby for their encouragement and love. Special thanks goes to my loving sons Derek, Daanen, and their wives, as well as my granddaughter Daria.

CREDENTIALS

The author has a B.S. Degree in Elementary Education. She holds a Master Degree in Early Childhood Education and has completed 36 hours towards a Ph.D. This educator taught K-3rd Grades in Dade County, Florida and was a dedicated, well-liked classroom teacher for 31 years. She retired in June 2004.

PILLER HIGH SCHOOL

I WAS FOURTEEN when I met Bobbie at Piller High School. I lived with my mama in a one-bedroom apartment. All my girlfriends had boyfriends except me, because mama told me to wait until I was seventeen. The moment I met Bobbie my heart told me not to wait. His soft-creamy-smooth skin and gorgeous brown eyes made my heart race out of control when we met. I tried to control my feelings for Bobbie, but I couldn't. I'd go to bed thinking about him. Is this the way love makes you feel I asked myself?

Bobbie was a senior at Piller and was a member of the Art Club. He was an excellent artist and painter who stayed after school to draw and paint with the other students. I played the clarinet in the band and stayed after school to practice, too. When our extra curricular activities were over, Bobbie and I would talk. Each time we met my feelings grew stronger and stronger for Bobbie. September 25th Bobbie asked me to be his girl. My heart skipped a beat and I quickly jumped into his arms. I didn't know how to tell Mama I was in love with Bobbie, so I kept it a secret.

Mama knew I was at band practice after school and I told her our sessions would be longer. This gave me private time with Bobbie. I had many friends that I hung out with in school and some of my best friends were boys. We would all laugh and play jokes on one another. I saw Bobbie and waved. The bell rang and it was time to go to class. After school I went to band practice and when it was over I waited for Bobbie. We met and went to his car. Bobbie had a red convertible Mustang. When I got into the car Bobbie started yelling at me. "Why were you laughing and talking to those boys? You're my girl. Bobbie's girl! "Don't talk to any guy but me," he said. Then he pushed me, pulled my hair and hit my thighs with his fist. I was horrified and scared. I started crying. He told me to shut up. I sat quietly as we drove to his apartment.

When we arrived at the apartment he pushed me again and pulled my hair and beat my thighs with his fists. I told him I was sorry. He told me he loved me and I believed him. He forced me to have sex with him and when it was over he took me close to home. I did not tell Mama what Bobbie had done. I told no one. This was my secret I did not share. It was hard to go to sleep because my thighs were sore. Finally I rubbed my thighs with alcohol and drifted off to sleep. Mama woke me to remind me it was time to go to Piller High.

DEPRESSION

S HE ASKED ME if I felt alright because I never overslept before. I told her I was up late reading and she accepted that. I just couldn't tell mama what Bobbie had done to me. It was hard for me to focus in class after my encounter with Bobbie and I had to tell myself, hold on to your strength and keep going forward. I began to feel depressed and couldn't stay around my friends too long. I was afraid Bobbie would see me with my friends and I found myself alone.

My friends didn't ask me what was going on and I told them nothing. Again I met Bobbie after band practice and rode in his convertible Mustang. He seemed happy as we drove around town. Today, we walked hand-in-hand to the ice cream parlor and shared ice cream and were off to a smooth start. Band practice was fun the next day and I felt like myself again. I was laughing and talking to a classmate when my eyes saw two girls arguing in the hallway. Several girls had gathered around them as they argued over a boy named Lance.

They found out Lance was going with both of them. They began to throw punches at each other and no one stopped them. I ran and told two teachers. There was so much screaming and yelling between the two that the teachers went through the crowd. They stopped the fight and the girls had to go to the principal's office. The school bell rang. Ring, ring and it was time to go to band practice. Bobbie's art class was canceled and I did not see him. I went straight home and finished my homework. I took my Rat Terrier for a walk and returned home before night had shown its face. Mama was driving in the driveway smiling happily. Later we ate dinner and had time to spend together with my dog. Night had fallen and it was almost time to go to bed. I practiced songs on my clarinet until I got sleepy. I woke up early and dressed for Piller High. Piller was having a dance show of different ethnic groups.

The dancers were great and the audience loved them. The school day ended and I went to band practice. I saw Bobbie and sat in my assigned seat. I couldn't wait to see him as I looked at the clock on the wall. Band was over and we walked out the door behind the other students. We went to the park and not to his apartment. We smelled and looked at the beautiful flowers that were in bloom as we held hands and walked. He told me he wanted to show me another side of him.

We had fun smelling flowers and running after each other. Bobbie later took me near home and I ran inside the apartment. I cooked a chicken dinner for mama and me. I wanted to surprise her because she took good care of my Rat Terrier and me. I loved mama so much and yet I couldn't tell mama what Bobbie was doing to me. My heart loved Bobbie. I wanted him to be my secret lover forever. Today was a teacher workday and mama knew it.

She left chores for me to do. When mama left for work I started on my chores. I cleaned the bathroom and washed two loads of clothes. My bed was made and the dishes were washed, too. I walked my dog and had lunch. Bobbie and I planned to meet each other for one hour. I walked a block and met Bobbie. I was a little late and he did not like that. "You know I don't like waiting," he told me. I apologized for being late and I thought he'd be O. K. with that. Bobbie did not forget I was late meeting him.

He punched my back and pulled my hair like he did before. I cried and he told me to be quiet and pose on the stool. I sat on the stool and he punched my back some more. Our session ended and Bobbie dropped me off close to my apartment. I went to my room full of pain and played my clarinet. I played songs over and over until I was happy with what I heard. My Rat Terrier seemed to enjoy my music, too. It was night when I finished my homework and looked out the window.

It started to thunder and the rain drops poked my window pane. Still in pain, I drew the curtains together and hopped on my bed. Soon I went to sleep. My dog jumped on my bed the next morning and I knew it was time to go to school. Homework was assigned again in two classes and soon it was time for lunch. Mama had to come for a teacher conference to see if I were failing or struggling in my classes. She was pleased with my progress in my classes. She told me to keep up the good work. One of my best girlfriends was Rita. She played clarinet in the band with me. Rita had long beautiful red hair and I asked her why didn't she cut it? She said she liked long hair and never had a haircut. I told her she could donate her locks to girls and women who lost their hair to chemo. She thought that was a good idea. Several days later Rita came to school with short hair. She looked beautiful and felt very happy and everyone in band was shocked to see the new Rita. When the girls in class found out why Rita cut her hair they wanted to donate their locks to this great cause. I also had cut my hair before I met Bobbie and donated my locks to women and girls who lost their hair to chemo.

Before I knew it, band practice was over. Then I saw Bobbie standing outside the open door. My heart sank. I told Bobbie mama was waiting outside to take me shopping and I could not see him. He said "O. K." and I went to mama and she dropped me home and she went to the store. Bobbie bought me my private telephone and I did not let mama know this. The phone rang and I picked it up to answer Bobbie's call. Again my heart sank because I did not know what Bobbie would say.

Reluctantly I said "hello". "Why didn't you tell me earlier that you were going shopping with your mother? You missed your photo session and now you've put me behind schedule. You know I'm an Artist and what I do. You better have your little ass in session tomorrow girlie," he said. I said "O. K." He threw the phone on the receiver. Bam! The next morning I woke up early and was excited to go to school again. I had done my Math and English assignments in my classes before going to band practice.

BEHIND SCHEDULE

I WAITED FOR the students to walk out the door and this gave me time to think about Bobbie Tutt. I went home and listened to my favorite rock songs and danced alone. I was thinking if Bobbie were with me, we could have a wonderful time. I wondered if he could dance because he never danced with me. I was afraid to ask him. All kinds of thoughts entered my mind about dancing with my secret lover. I imagined myself dancing with Bobbie at my prom. Then I did not know if he wanted to go to the prom, or would he let me go to the prom.

My mind flashed back to our first kiss. It was wonderful and I put all negative thoughts about Bobbie out of my mind. He was implanted in my heart and soul. We practiced our songs in school and left the band class. I took my Rat Terrier for a long walk and returned home before night had fallen. Mama's car was parked in the driveway. She bought food to eat and that gave us time to spend together. Night was upon us and it was almost time to go to bed.

I practiced songs on my clarinet and mama took pictures of me playing my clarinet and the Rat Terrier singing as I played. Mama laughed and laughed. We told each other good night and went to bed. I woke up early and dressed for school. It started to rain when the students walked into the door of the school. Everyone walked swiftly to their classes and they were happy to get inside. I went to my English class and copied the homework assignments down. We had to write a poem about the rain.

When class was over we turned our papers in and went to the next class. Soon it was time to go home. I set the dinner table for mama and she prepared dinner. The next morning I went to school with a smile on my face. I called mama and told her I was staying late at band practice.

Bobbie and I drove to his apartment and he was quiet. I felt something was brewing in his head and I kept quiet, too. His face turned red as he yelled. "I am behind schedule with my work." He pulled my hair and gave me several blows to my back.

I felt the stinging on my back as I sat sobbing. We entered the apartment and he told me to stop crying and wash my face. I went into the bathroom and washed my face and combed my hair. I put makeup on Bobbie had for me and stripped off my clothes. Naked from head to toe I sat and posed on the stool. Bobbie spun the stool around and looked at my stinging back. "Your back isn't painting ready he uttered." Yet I posed and accepted the hits he placed on my sore back with his fists. I cried and cried. When it was over I dried my tears and reapplied my make-up. Soon the session was over. We had sex and talked in bed. Bobbie told me he loved me and I was the girl for him. He said he was going to be everybody's Artist and they were going to buy his paintings. Bobbie told me he was the number one Artist in class and his work was rated A1A by his teacher.

We got out of bed and he showed me some of his paintings that he had done in Art class. He learned art from his dad before he and his mom divorced. He was going to enlarge his studio to hold more paintings he told me. "Your back will be beautiful and your paintings will be a big seller" he stated. "Never do something and not finish it" he told me as he looked at me with those beautiful brown eyes. "I said "O.K." It was time to go home and my brown-eyed lover took me near the place I lived.

I ran inside still feeling the pain Bobbie inflicted on my back. Mama was not home from work and I fell across the bed sobbing. I cried and forced myself to forget the nightmare I had experienced. I heard mama turn the key into the door. When she got inside she called my name.

"Coffee", she yelled. "Yes," I answered. Mama cooked a quick dinner and I washed the dishes. The next day I saw Bobbie before band practice began and told him I was spending the weekend with my dad.

I hadn't seen daddy in years I told him. Hoping Bobbie would understand he screamed "What?" Everyone turned around. He walked away and said "sure". I sat down with the band members and started to play Piper Stars and Strings. Band practice ended and I called daddy on the phone. He said he couldn't see me this weekend but I could visit him the following weekend. I didn't tell Bobbie my visit with daddy was canceled. I felt like a liar and a person no one could trust.

DADDY'S VISIT

I WANTED TO call Bobbie on the phone but my heart and the pains on my back wouldn't let me. I changed the thoughts in my head. The next week I called daddy on the phone again. Finally he answered the phone and we talked. He told me to come and meet his family. Mama drove me to daddy's house. She looked at me and I looked at her. We saw this big two-story stucco house with a two car garage. She told me to relax and have fun and drove away. I stood and looked at this beautiful house and wondered what it looked like inside.

I was nervous as I looked at the cars in the driveway. I saw the beautiful flowers and green grass along the sidewalk. I wondered were the people as beautiful as the house, or was I walking into a nightmare. I remembered mama told me to relax before she left and I took a deep breath and rang the doorbell. Ring and the door opened and a tall man called my name and I knew I was at the right house. He held my hands and kissed me on the cheek. His wife greeted me and I was introduced to my sister and brother for the first time.

I felt out of place with these people. All I could think about was my strong and wonderful mama, Bobbie and my adorable Rat Terrier. Somehow I settled down with daddy and his family. They showed me around the house and we went inside the large master bedroom. The drapes and paintings were gorgeous and so was the large marble bathroom. My sister and brother's rooms had characters of their own. My brother's room was filled with football paraphernalia and my sister was a fan of Kinky Bop.

We settled down in the living room and got to know one another. Ray's wife served a snack to everyone while we watched a movie. Before I knew it, night had fallen and it was time to go home to mama. Mama asked me about my visit with daddy. I told her it was fine and he wanted me to visit again. She was happy for me that he wanted me in his life. I was happy too. I woke up early for school and was happy it was a school day. The sun rose and mama was ready for work.

Last night mama told me about the town she lived in when she was a young girl. It was a small community where everyone knew one another. The town was called Race Lane. Some of the houses there were spread far apart because no one bought the lot next to that house. All the children knew one another because they rode the same school bus. There was this one girl named Laura who could not ride the school bus for long because Cindy would bully her everyday. Soon Laura stopped riding the school bus and her aunt had to drive her to school.

It happened that Laura's house was across from my house and we became good friends mama said. She came to see me and I went to see her. Laura loved the boys. I didn't know anything about boys, except I could recognize them. She had her eyes on a soldier boy. I got a job when I finished school and lost contact with Laura. I went back to the place I lived and found Laura. We still are good friends. My favorite day of the week was Saturday because mama and I could talk to each other. I wanted to ask her why she divorced daddy. I felt close to mama and yet my inner self couldn't tell her I had disobeyed her. I did not have the heart to tell mama I had a boyfriend named Bobbie Tutt. I loved Bobbie and I couldn't tell her about him.

MAMA TALKS

THIS SECRET BELONGED to me and only me. We had apple cake and tea as we sat at the dinner table. I asked mama why she divorced daddy. "Coffee, it's a long and painful story. Your daddy worked in construction and made enough money to take care of the bills we had. My checks were spent on me and he didn't have a problem with that. When his work got slow his attitude changed toward me. He started cursing at me because he did not have money to spend like he once had. His workdays were reduced to two days a week and he was out-of-control.

He was angry as a vicious bull when he came home from work. One night he beat me up. I had a black eye and bruises on my arms and neck. I had to go to the hospital. He was charged with abuse and served time in jail. I took him back and after a few months the beatings started again. He got another construction job and I thought he was happy. I went to work with bruises on my chest and legs. No one knew I was living in horror but me. One Saturday night he told me he wanted me to pay all the bills and he would be handling the checks.

He gave me the money he wanted me to have out of my checks. Sometime I had only gas money. I could not say or do anything about this as long as I lived with Ray. I use to buy myself pretty clothes and shoes until he controlled the money and my buying power went to nothing. There was a time I wanted to buy myself a pair of shoes because the ones I was wearing had loose soles. I did not have the money to buy them, so I had to put super glue on the bottom for them to stay together. It worked and I wore them to work with a smile on my face. I found myself saving every penny I got from Ray. From this experience I became frugal. I thought that if he took my checks the beatings would cease. I was wrong! Ray continued to drink and the beatings followed. One Friday night he pushed me against the dresser knob and the imprint of the knob was left on my back.

It was painful and I fell across the bed face down. I saw him walk out of the room and slam the door. All kinds of thoughts ran through my mind and I knew I was in a horrible situation. My dad always told me if a man loves you he would treat you like a princess. I knew from the beatings Ray was treating me like I was an old worn nasty rug on the floor. I thought of myself as an old worn rug that he did not want. But I stayed with Ray because I loved him and I did not have the money to leave.

Somehow I knew that I needed to do something. After three years of abuse I started going to church. They had guest counselors to speak about abusive relationships. I listened and told myself I was going to get out of the relationship with Ray. I went home and said nothing to your daddy. I realized I was living with a man that really didn't care about me. One September morning when Ray went to work, I went to work. I told my boss I was moving out-of-state. I took my check and went home and threw some clothes in the car. I wrote Ray a note telling him I was leaving him for good. Pots, pans and jewelry were left behind. I didn't care. I was on my way to start a new life with you. We lived in a shelter for homeless people for three months. When you went to school I looked for a job. I got a job and rented an apartment. When I got settled I made sure I gave money every month to homeless charities. I still visit the homeless shelter that we lived in and the people that were in the shelter with us were gone. I saw new faces at the shelter when I visited the other day.

They had counselors to help the women and men who had been abused and they even helped them get jobs which was wonderful. No one should be homeless or abused. This is my story Coffee. I heard mama's story and I just could not tell her my story. I went to my room and asked myself, "Why didn't you tell her?" "I just couldn't. I did not want to hurt her. I loved mama but my heart loved Bobbie Tutt more. My secret sealed my lips."

HE MISSED ME

IN SCHOOL I saw the usual gang before the bell rang. When school was over I went to band practice again. Bobbie was in art class painting a picture. When our practices were over we went to his Mustang and he told me he missed and loved me. He held my hands tightly. "Wow!" Was I glad to hear those words from Bobbie. I told him I loved him and missed him too. In his apartment Bobbie started yelling at me again. "Don't ever stay away from me again, Bitch," he said. He threw me on the bed and kissed me passionately.

He grabbed my feet and punched my toes so hard that my pinkie snapped. I cried "stop! Bobbie, stop!" He called me a cry baby and began hitting my back. When he finished he told me to put fresh makeup on, strip and sit on the damn stool. I was terrified. I told Bobbie my pinkie was hurting and he said he didn't care. I was in pain. I dried my tears and calmly sat on the stool. He wiped my face and applied make-up to my young face. With each touch and stroke on my back I felt the pain.

Yet I accepted what Bobbie was doing to me because I loved him. Soon it was over and time to go home. He'd drop me off not too far from home. I went straight to my room and fell asleep on the bed. The next morning I got ready for school and was happy to see my friends at Piller High. Classes were over and you could hear the loud laughter from the students as you walked passed them. When I got home I thought about daddy. I waited for his phone call. Finally the phone rang and I thought to myself, was it Bobbie? Or was it daddy? I picked up the phone and it was daddy. I was glad! Daddy and I talked and talked. At the end of our conversation he invited me to come over Saturday and have dinner with him. "We are having a fish-fry cookout and have invited a few friends over. "O.K." I replied. "Great!" When mama got home I told her daddy invited me over for a fish-fry dinner. "That's good," she uttered.

I ran to my room and looked out the window. The sky was a gorgeous reddish-orange and the stars were a bright yellow. As I gazed at the night sky I felt peace and happiness come over me. My soft satin pillow anxiously wanted my head to be placed upon it. I drifted off to sleep and woke up in time for school. The teacher started the day off with homework assignments. I saw Bobbie at band practice as I sat in my assigned seat. Again we met when our classes were over. When we arrived at Bobbie's apartment he was ready to paint me.

He told me there was a good movie playing Friday. "Would you like to go?" he asked. "I cannot go because daddy is having a fish-fry at his house." "Fish-fry!" he yelled. "You're turning me down over a fish-fry." He was furious! He pulled my hair and beat my back. I screamed, "Bobbie you're hurting me. Stop hitting my back." "Don't tell me what to do," he yelled back. He continued beating my back and there was nothing I could do. I cried and fell off the stool and got up and sat back on the stool and sobbed. He spun the stool around and began spray painting and painting my sore back. He pushed me off the stool and dragged me on the bed. I knew what was coming next and did not say a word to him. He slapped my thighs and pinned my arms behind my back. He raped me again and we went to sleep. When I awoke I told Bobbie I had to leave before mama got home. I got home in time before mama arrived.

I cooked dinner like I usually did for mama. I did my homework and listened to music before going to sleep. The next day I did not see Bobbie because his art class was canceled. I went home and talked to daddy on the phone. The next morning the weather was cool when I left for school and my classmates had a new tone in their voices as they walked down the hall. I went to band practice when my last class ended and I saw my brown-eyed lover. We walked hand-in-hand to his Mustang and he was in a happy mood. He stopped at the corner store and bought hot dogs and sodas.

We finished the snacks in his apartment. Bobbie was happy and I was happy. We were happy lovers I thought.

He showed me the beautiful paints in the trays. He said, "This is my gold and without them I would not make a living." "You are my model." "You are my lovely model." "I need you to paint and let's get started." I started to take off my clothes not fast enough for him. He smacked my back and told me to hurry up. My back was still sore from the previous hits. I screamed and he told me to close my mouth.

FURIOUS BOBBIE

H E PULLED MY hair and grabbed my face and said "Shut up. Shut up." I stopped screaming and did what Bobbie told me to do. He spray painted the middle of my back and I sat and did not say anything to him. He waited for the paint to dry and when the paint dried he took me near home. I arrived home and mama was waiting for me. Mama asked me why I was late. I lied and told her practice did not start on time and that's why I was late. She believed me and no more questions were asked.

I did not want to lie to mama but I couldn't tell her my secret. Mama loved to hear me play the clarinet and I played some of her favorite songs for her. It turned dark and the sky looked reddish-orange again. I gazed at the night sky. The orange glow was so strong I fell asleep and when I woke up I realized I slept in my clothes. It was time for school. My English teacher gave us homework and so did my math teacher. We were given literature homework too. I skipped P.E. and did some of my homework.

I did not want to miss a session with Bobbie. I loved Bobbie so much that I would do anything for him and he knew it. School was over for the day and band and art classes were not held. I went home without holding my lover's hand. Mama cooked dinner and that gave me time to finish my homework. Out side the window the sky was dark and dreary. I went to bed and hugged my pillow and Rat Terrier. I drifted off to sleep. Bobbie was biting my breasts and arms. He was beating my legs with a belt and I woke up screaming. "Eek! Eek!" I looked around and realized I was dreaming. Mama ran into the bedroom and asked me what was wrong.

It was a bad dream I told her. She stayed in the room with me for a while before going back to bed.

It was hard for me to go back to sleep. The next thing I knew it was time for school. It was early dismissal day and I went to band practice again. I did not sit in my assigned seat. Instead I sat in the empty seat in the back of the room and went to sleep. I heard someone call my name saying "Wake up Coffee." It was the band instructor. I felt embarrassed! This will never happen again I told him. He walked away and said nothing. The entire room was quiet. Bobbie saw me and we left the class together. "I saw you sleep in class," he said. "Were you out all night?" "No," I told him. I would not tell him about the nightmare I had about him.

He did not say any more about me sleeping in practice. When we got to his apartment my legs started shaking and tears ran down my face. In an angry voice he said, "Dry your tears girl and put on your makeup." His order was obeyed. I sat there grinding my teeth as I felt each stroke of the paint brush on my back. "A few more bruises and your back will be an artist' dream, he told me. "We will work again tomorrow." "Let me drop you off not too far from your apartment Coffee." Yes, I will always think of myself as Bobbie's Girl because he is a snapshot of my first love and the memory of him has been implanted in my heart forever.

Halloween had arrived and mama and I were getting ready for the little ones. We had lots of candy for them when they knocked on the door. They got their treats and wished us a happy Halloween. We closed the door and mama told me some children do have good manners. I didn't talk to Bobbie on Halloween because he told me he didn't have time for such foolishness. "I'm too busy painting and I do not answer my door on Halloween," he said. He stressed that he was above and beyond such celebration. I did not question him because I was afraid to and he told me not to question him.

All I wanted was harmony and love between Bobbie and me. I did not go out to trick or treat because I had homework to do. We celebrated Halloween by decorating our apartment in orange and black. Mama never threw away my Halloween costumes when I was a little girl. We hung the costumes around the apartment to celebrate the scary occasion. We watched a Halloween horror flick before going to bed. My Rat Terrier had keen ears as he heard the screams of the children as they went from apartment to apartment yelling "Trick or Treat."

He kept barking until the children left. What a crazy night it was for us. The next day I saw my brown-eyed lover in class. All the students in art had to bring in a project. Each student had to show and tell about the project he or she made. One girl in Art class created her own doll that walked around the room. Everyone seemed to like her project. In our Music class we had to challenge one another on songs that were selected by the teacher. We also had to write a song and play it for the class and that song was graded by the teacher.

The class voted on the best song and the students were given the notes to that song and everyone played it together. Our students were having lots of fun and did not want to stop playing the songs. Before class ended we had a book of songs we could practice. I looked over in Bobbie's Art class and he was presenting his project to the class. Bobbie had made and painted a skateboard. His pictures were so magnificent that everyone clapped for him.

He started explaining his project and every eye was fixed on him. The teacher asked him to leave his work in class so that all the Art students could see his work. The bell rang and the classes were over. Bobbie and I walked out the door holding hands and he went home alone. I did not go with Bobbie because he did not ask me to. Mama picked me up from Music class and she decided that we were not going to cook tonight. We went to a small eatery and enjoyed dinner. Mama told me it was time for me to buy new clothes and she took me shopping at the mall. Mama bought me a pair of shoes and a pretty skirt and blouse. I bought an outfit for my Rat Terrier.

Mama asked me if I had decided on a name for it. I did not have a name for my dog and I agreed that it should have a name. I told her I would juggle some names in my head and come up with a name for my pet. We left the mall and headed home to our apartment. My dog heard the key turn in the door knob as we entered the apartment.

DADDY'S PLEA FOR HELP

I T WAS SO glad to see us that it jumped into my arms and licked my face. It jumped down and did the same thing to mama. We had a wonderful night before going to bed. The neighbors were quiet and the moon moved across the dark sky. School would soon be over in a few months. Most of the students talked about summer vacation and family gathering. I thought about Bobbie and the time we would spend together secretly. I never met his mom and thought this might be a good time to do so.

All kinds of thoughts were thrilling in my head as what Bobbie and I would do after my back was finished. Bobbie was everything I wanted in a man. I loved him so much that I wanted to be with him all the time. I only saw myself in his arms and his fast red Mustang convertible. He was my love and he had the ride I adored. I didn't want him to have another girl because I was Bobbie's girl. Bobbie and I met again. Everything was cool as we rode in his car. He told me he enjoyed painting and I told him about my favorite subjects and my playful Rat Terrier.

"Let's get to work," he told me as we entered his abode. He grabbed a clothespin from the easel and pinched my back in different places. I screamed "EEK!" "Bobbie, that hurts." I yelled. He didn't listen to me. He hit and punched my back with the clothespin again and again and then he stopped and kissed my aching back. Slowly he spun the stool around and spray painted my back again. He took colored magic markers and paint to make pictures from the bruises on my back. My back was sore when the camera flashed and flashed. Bobbie Tutt the painter had the biggest smile on his face as he sprayed and painted. It looked as if he was in another world. I posed and posed my naked body on the stool for Bobbie. The camera stopped flashing and it was over. Bobbie had finished the painting on my back. He took me near home in his convertible Mustang.

I lay across the bed and fell asleep. When I awoke my back was still sore and I realized I slept in my clothes again. I took a large mirror and held it in front of me as I stood with my back facing the tall mirror on the wall. I saw the painting on my back. It was beautiful! It was gorgeous! I'd never seen a painting like it before. It was different. It was one of a kind painting and I was the only person in the world who had a painting like that. I wanted to show mama the beautiful painting on my back but I couldn't.

She didn't know I had a boyfriend let alone a lover. So I kept my back a secret. This secret belonged to Bobbie and me. Now I knew why Bobbie's paintings in school was graded A1A. I kept looking at my beautiful back in the mirror and felt Leonardo couldn't top the painting on my back. I lay down on my satin sheet and pillow case and went to sleep. I was a beautiful model showing off the painting on my back. Everyone wanted me to model low-cut bathing suits and gowns showing off the painting on my beautiful back.

I made lots of money and my pictures were on every store front. I had my own private jet and traveled to London and Paris. I modeled and modeled because everybody wanted to see my beautiful back as I walked and turned on the runway. My pictures were in all the magazines and plastered on the front of buses in Paris and London. I woke up and realized I was dreaming. I looked at the clock and it was nearing eight. I put on my best skirt and blouse and I told mama I was ready to see daddy. She said I looked pretty and drove me to daddy's house.

Enjoy yourself she told me as she left. I rang the door bell and my sister and brother said hi. Daddy and his wife were happy to see me and walked me to the backyard and he introduced me to the people in the yard. He cooked lots of food for everybody. I soon joined my sister and brother upstairs to play monopoly and got to know them better.

PICTURES

THEN EVERYBODY WAS called to eat and afterward we took pictures together like one happy family. I got to see another side of daddy. Mama told me daddy was abusive and that's why she left him. Something happened to daddy because he appeared happy with his new wife and family. Oh well mama moved on with her life. The party was over and I had to go home to see my mama. I told my sister, brother, daddy and his wife I had a good time as they walked me to the door. Mama was waiting outside for me and we went home.

Bobbie told me the next day he needed to take more pictures of my back. I kissed him and said, "I'm yours." Tutt whispered, "You were always what I wanted" and took more pictures of my naked body and back. He took picture after picture and posted them on the internet. I saw the orders he was getting and the money he was making. "You're going to be a famous artist I told him." I loved Bobbie with all my heart and soul. Before I met Bobbie Tutt I wanted to go to college out-of-state.

I realized I had to change my mind and attend a college near home. I loved this boy and was caught in the web of his gorgeous brown eyes. I was trapped at the age of fourteen. Each day passed by I wanted to see Bobbie more and more. He was my brown-eyed secret lover and companion. I stared at the wall knowing that he couldn't be with me because of the secret we couldn't tell. I wanted to have a diary but I was afraid mama would find it. I changed my mind about having a diary as some girls do. Bobbie would be best in my heart than my diary I thought. I was ready for school because it was exam week. Our music classes sold pizza and sodas after school to buy new band uniforms. We made lots of money and were soon able to buy new uniforms. Everyone was excited when the uniforms came.

I took my new uniform home for mama to see and she was excited too. The next morning I returned the uniform and rushed to my English class. School was over and I went home and read Shakespeare. Before I knew it night had fallen and I was finishing my homework. I played with my dog and called it a night. The next evening I visited daddy and his family. He took us to a local restaurant for dinner. We all were enjoying our dinner when an angry customer started arguing with the waitress because his food was cold.

He was loud and the manager talked to the angry man. The man wanted his money returned and the manager gave the guy his money and he left the restaurant. Later we left the restaurant and stopped at the ice cream parlor. Bobbie brought me to this ice cream parlor and I did not tell daddy this. We all had a great time and returned to his house. Everyone told me they wanted me to spend the night the next time over. My siblings and stepmother went upstairs. Daddy put his arms around me and gave me a tight hug.

I felt the horrible pain across my back and screamed "EEK!" and dropped to the floor. He was scared and asked me what was wrong. I told him my back was sore and he suggested I stand and turn around. He asked me to raise my blouse from the back making sure my blouse covered my small breasts. I did as daddy commanded. He was petrified at what he saw. Daddy asked, "Who put the bruises on your back Coffee?" "I told him it was a painting. He yelled, "Painting my eye." "Who put the bruises on your back?" He asked again. I had to tell daddy. Finally I said "Bobbie Tutt."

"Who is Bobbie Tutt?" He asked. "My boyfriend at Piller High" I replied. "Bobbie raped me." "Raped you?" "I'm calling the police" he said in an angry voice. Shaking all over I said "Daddy please, please don't call the cops." "Daddy please, please, do not call the police on Bobbie. I love Bobbie. He is my world and the boy I adore. I'm everything to him and he's everything to me. Bobbie is my secret lover and I love him daddy. I love him! Please don't call the police" I begged.

Daddy said, Coffee this is a secret I cannot keep. The police must know what Bobbie has done to you. Coffee you have been abused. You are a minor. You're my child and I see your mother in you. I did the same thing to your mama as Bobbie has done to you. I had to go to jail for hurting your mama and Bobbie must pay for what he has done to you. Coffee you are only fourteen." Daddy called the police. He told mama to come inside and he showed her my sore and bruised back. She too was petrified at what she saw. Tears formed in mama's eyes and daddy told her who Bobbie Tutt was and what he had done to me. "Why did you keep everything a secret from me Coffee?" Mama asked. "I told you my secret and you didn't tell me yours." "I didn't want to hurt mama. I just couldn't tell anyone my secret not even you. Help me mama!" I hugged mama tightly. I took daddy and the police to Bobbie's apartment and he was shocked to see us. Then and there Bobbie Tutt was handcuffed and arrested. Bobbie's arrest spread like wildfire. The media was all over the story and that was the last time I saw Bobbie. I learned Bobbie had decided to dump me for another girl. He was making money on the web with my paintings and his website was pulled from the internet. He would have abused another girl if I had not told daddy. Bobbie will be in prison for a long time. Coffee has received group counseling and therapy. She continues to go to school.

AUTHOR'S MESSAGE

ABUSE IS NOT a pretty color. A red, black, purple, blue, yellow, or pink mark on your body is painful. According to Webster's Dictionary abuse means to be ill-treated, insulted, mistreated, defamed and misused. Abuse is not alright. It is not acceptable. No one should be mistreated. Not even a dog. Listen, everyone! My dad was a weekend alcoholic when he inflicted bruises on my mother's leg. When my brother and I became teenagers we told daddy not to hit mama again. We warned him if he didn't stop we were going to hit him.

He stopped drinking and the abuse ended. I was five years old when my dad abused my mother and I never forgot what I saw and the pain she endured. I felt her pain too. Anyone that is in an abusive relationship should SEEK HELP. The National Domestic Violence Hotline provides help to callers 365 days a year, 24 hours a day. The National Domestic Violence Hotline Advocates are there for victims and anyone calling on someone else's behalf to give information, safety planning, referrals and crisis intervention. They have referrals to agencies in 50 states including Puerto Rico and the U.S. Virgin Islands. Help can be given in Spanish and English. The National Domestic Violence Hotline has access to more than 170 languages through interpreter services.

IF YOU OR SOMEONE YOU KNOW IS BEING ABUSED CALL THE NATIONAL DOMESTIC VIOLENCE HOTLINE AT 1-800-799 SAFE (7233) OR TTY-1800-787-3224.

The **National Teen Dating Abuse Helpline, loveisrespect.org** is a 24-hour resource for teens and young adults experiencing dating abuse. It is specifically designed with teens and young adults in mind, operating around the growing technologies that they use most often: the phone, the web, and chat. Young men and women, along with their friends and families, can anonymously contact a trained teen dating abuse advocate by phone 24/7 at **1-866-331-9474 or TTY (866) 331-8453.** They can also chat in one-on-one, confidential conversation with a peer advocate between the hours of 4 p.m. and 2 a.m.

All advocates on the National Teen Dating Abuse Helpline, loveisrespect.org are trained to offer crisis intervention, safety planning, and referrals from a database of over 4,500 resource providers.

READERS THOUGHTS AND OPINIONS

1. What mistakes did Coffee make?

2. Would your decisions be the same as Coffee's or would they be different? Explain.

3. Now that Coffee's receiving group counseling and therapy, what do you think Coffee's life will be like now?

4. Have you ever been in an abusive situation? If your answer is yes, please explain what happened to you.

5. How did you solve your abusive problem(s)? What help did you get? Have all these experiences been erased from your mind? Elaborate.

6. Do you think everyone needs to know The National Domestic Violence Hotline number? Or, the National Teen Dating Abuse Helpline,loveisrespect.org. Explain your answer.

SYNOPSIS

BOBBIE'S GIRL IS a heart-wrenching love story about a fourteen year-old girl and a seventeen year-old boy who fall secretly in love.

Coffee's quest for love takes her on an unbelievable journey. Their torrid relationship is full of abuse and she tells no one. Not even her mother. This was Coffee's secret.

Mesmerized by Bobbie's soft-creamy-smooth skin and convertible Mustang, Coffee rode herself into an apartment full of despicable abuse, control and secrecy. She's willing to accept his abuse in order to hold on to her first love.

This incredible love story shows the consequences of not reporting abuse and the pain and suffering Coffee endured.

In the end Coffee halts her journey of abuse when she discloses the face of her abuser.

Printed in the United States
By Bookmasters